DATE DUE

12/07

This is the story of a little boy called Magnus. When he was seven years old, he and his family made the long journey from Greenland to Vinland in order to settle there.

Magnus the Viking
Original title: Magnus Viking™

©Egmont Bøker Fredhøi AS - SFG
N-0055 Oslo
www.touristbooks.com

Author: Frid Ingulstad
Illustrated by Digital Fortellerteknikk
Design: Skomsøy Grønli AS
Translations: Berlitz GlobalNET
Printed in Denmark by Nørhaven AS

Magnus the Viking

by
Frid Ingulstad

Illustrated by
Asbjørn Tønnesen

t last they were ready to go! Magnus ran excitedly down to the three large ships which were to take them across the ocean to Vinland, the new land discovered by Leif. He clambered on board the largest ship. Just think – they would be almost the first people to arrive in this new land. But Leif had said that some brown, almost naked people lived in the forest there. Magnus thought this sounded very exciting.

Soon everyone was aboard, and the ship slipped slowly out into the bay.

Father stood at the rudder looking very strong and powerful. By the holes for the oars along either side of the ship there were trunks for the crew to sit on as they rowed, and inside these trunks all their clothes were stored.

In the middle of the boat were their cows, horses and sheep. The boat was packed full of barrels of dried fish, cured meat and the men's leather sacks containing their weapons. They had bows and arrows, swords and battle axes.

5

Magnus went up to old Olve, who was a sorcerer. Olve could conjure up rain or sunshine, whichever was needed. He did not believe in the White Christ – the god in whom Magnus' mother and father believed. Olve and many of the others worshipped Odin and Thor, the old gods. Odin was a god with only one eye. He had given up the other one in order to become wise. When the men were going on a Viking raid, they sacrificed animals to Odin so that he would help them in battle. Olve had told Magnus that in some places they even sacrificed people. Magnus didn't like to think about this, but he loved listening to everything else Olve told him.

Suddenly Magnus felt a gust of wind. At that moment, Father gave the order to hoist the sail and the oars were drawn in. All the shields which had been hung on the outside of the ship were now taken in so that they would not be torn away by the waves.

For the first two days and nights of the journey, as they travelled northwards up the coast of Greenland, everything went fine. But then, when they turned westwards and lost sight of the land, the weather turned stormy. The wind whined and moaned, and dark clouds drove down from the north. All of a sudden Magnus felt an ominous atmosphere.

Sigrid, one of the servant women, looked up at the sky. "The storm is coming from Jotunland!" she whispered.

"Oh," cried Magnus, scared. "Where is Jotunland?"

"It's where the trolls live," whispered Sigrid. She did not want Magnus' mother to hear her. "They are huge, dangerous giants, and they can only be killed by means of sorcery," she continued. "But they can be killed by the sword, at least with a troll sword like Olve has."

Magnus looked at Olve. It was reassuring to know that he had his troll sword at the ready in his leather sack, just in case a troll should come marching out of the skies!

"They live in a land far, far to the North, and do not usually mingle with humans," Sigrid continued. "But sometimes they come down to us. Then they live in caves or inside the mountains, and if you're out at night, you can hear branches rustling and twigs breaking as they step on them."

The wind began to blow a gale. Magnus peered around nervously. It was as black as night. The waves were dark and threatening. The wind whistled in the mast and the ropes, shrieking and howling. The ship creaked ominously and the rain beat on his face like nails of ice.

The frightened horses, cows and sheep huddled closely together in the keel of the ship where they sought shelter. The crew held on tightly and stared at the enormous waves which rose up before them like huge mountains. Some of them prayed to God, while others prayed to the old god, Thor, who had power over the thunder and lightning.

Magnus glanced anxiously up at the heavy sky. At that precise moment the lightning struck right above them, and he huddled up tightly. Up there, Thor was driving his wagon drawn by two goats. Each time the thunder crashed, it was Thor furiously brandishing his hammer in the air!

He heard the men call out something, but their voices were drowned by the raging storm. The foaming sea lashed on board, threatening to fill the boat, and the men bailed for all they were worth, while their hair and beards became white with the freezing spray. Magnus was so cold that his teeth chattered uncontrollably. The rain had seeped into his cloak and he was wet through to the skin.

Now and then, as the ship plunged down between the waves, he caught a glimpse of something large and dark, and realised that it was one of the other two ships. At other times he saw something large and white, and when he called out to his mother to ask what it was, she shouted back that it was an iceberg.

Through the pouring rain he saw that men were beginning to throw things overboard, and he knew that this was to make sure that they did not capsize.

"Are we going to die, Mamma?" he called out fearfully. But no-one answered.

At that moment he heard a shriek above the storm. He caught a fleeting glimpse of a dark figure disappearing over the rail and sinking into the stormy sea. It was one of the men who had fallen overboard. One of the others tried to grab hold of him before he disappeared, but he was too late.

The storm continued all that day and Magnus lay frightened and trembling from the cold, sheltering under one of the shields. But he did not cry. He seldom did so. In any case no-one would have heard him. Mother found one of the leather sacks which they used to sleep in at night, and Magnus crept inside it. He lay there thinking about everything he had heard about people drowning at sea. He wondered what it would feel like if the boat suddenly tipped over and everyone slid into the deep black water. It was such a terrible thought that he cast it out of his mind.

Finally, in the afternoon of the second day, the wind began to drop, the rain ceased, and Magnus crept out of the leather sack.

"What a brave boy you are," said Mother.

Eleven days after they had left Greenland, they caught sight of their new homeland. The air was clear and surprisingly warm, and the sun shone over the blue sea speckled with icebergs and green islands.

On board everyone stared solemnly towards the shore.

"Just think! We're almost the first people ever to come to this land!" cried Mother enthusiastically.

The three proud Viking ships sailed in between the islands and the rocks, their sails flapping gently in the breeze. They were approaching a broad sandy bay behind which there was a large green meadow. Magnus could hardly wait to get ashore and run straight up the hill to the forest beyond.

Then they saw the cabins which Leif had built. Father said that he had called them "Leif's cabins". There was one large dwelling near the beach, and several smaller ones in the meadow behind.

Magnus was one of the very first people to get ashore. He ran excitedly towards the green grassy meadow. The sun was shining, the air was warm, and he was so happy to be able to use his legs again at long last! He ran straight up to the first house. It was just like the longhouse at home, except that it was built of turf and timber instead of stone.

Mother followed him and unlocked the door with the keys which Leif had given her. They entered a large room with open hearths in the middle of the floor and benches for beds along the two longest walls. The floor was made of earth which had been trampled down hard. They looked round their new home in amazement.

Then Magnus ran down to the boats again and helped the grown-ups carry all the stores up to the cabins. Finally, when everything had been brought ashore, the ship was laid on its side on the beach so that the animals could jump into the shallow water and wade ashore.

Magnus slept like a log that night. At last he could sleep in a bed which did not swing from side to side.

In the days which followed, the grown-ups were very busy and Magnus wandered around exploring. Sometimes he ran up to the smithy and watched the blacksmith making weapons, and sometimes he peered into the oven where the charcoal was made. Both the smithy and the charcoal burner were located well away from the other cabins so that any sparks would not start a fire.

But most of all Magnus liked the forest. It reminded him of Norway where he had lived for the first few years of his life. He jumped excitedly from one hummock to the next, clambering over large branches, hopping over twigs and running through the heather.

One day when Magnus was out in the forest he suddenly heard a branch snapping. For a moment he froze with fright. Perhaps there were trolls here in this new land as well? But no, that was ridiculous. The sound was far too faint to have been made by a huge troll. It must have been an animal. Cautiously he made his way to the place where he had heard the sound come from.

In front of him the forest opened out into a small glade, and in the middle of a grassy bank stood … a little boy! A boy about the same size as himself. The boy had brown skin and black hair, and was wearing nothing but a strip of leather around his loins. On his back he had a quiver of arrows, and in his hand he held a fine bow.

Magnus held his breath, full of excitement. This boy must be one of the children of the wild people Leif had talked about! He squatted as still as a mouse. The boy raised his bow and aimed towards a large tree. He drew the bow and fired. The arrow streaked through the air and hit the tree trunk with a thud. The boy uttered a cry of joy and ran to the tree to retrieve the arrow. Now Magnus had become so eager that he dared to creep a bit closer. Just then the boy caught sight of him. For a moment they both stood frozen to the spot, staring at each other, and then the boy spun round and disappeared between the trees.

Magnus stayed where he was for a short while. He really wanted to find out more about this strange boy, but Leif had said that these people were dangerous. And after all, Leif's brother had been killed by one of their arrows.

To think that he was the first person to have seen one of them properly! Magnus was about to run home and tell Father about it, when he decided against this. If he told them, they would certainly not allow him to go into the forest alone any more, and he would never see this strange boy again.

In fact, the boy did not appear to be so very different from any other children, except that he had black hair and wore hardly any clothes. Magnus did not have anyone to play with, as there were no other children at Leif's cabins. And this boy had a bow and arrow exactly like his own. What fun it would be to see who could fire arrows furthest!

Magnus went around all day thinking about this stranger. When he went to bed that night he desperately wanted to tell his mother, but he managed not to say anything. The next day he went back to the same place, full of suspense, and to his great surprise he saw the other boy there again. When the boy saw Magnus he stood and looked inquisitively at him for a while before disappearing into the forest again. Perhaps he did not have anyone to play with either, thought Magnus, and decided to come back the following day as well.

The same thing happened for three days in a row, but on the fourth day Magnus had a bright idea. He wore his wooden sword in its sheath around his waist and held his bow and arrow in his hand. When the boy appeared, Magnus raised his bow and aimed at a tree. He drew the bow and fired. But he missed, and the arrow disappeared between the trees. Magnus turned towards the boy and smiled sheepishly.

The boy raised his bow, aimed at the same tree – and hit it! He shot a pleased look at Magnus, and Magnus, still a bit embarrassed, smiled admiringly. "Here," he said, handing the boy his bow. "Try mine."

The boy stood and stared at him for a while, not understanding. He had certainly not understood the language, but after a while he realised what Magnus meant. Cautiously, he took the bow and fired. He made a direct hit this time too.

"You're really good," said Magnus, full of admiration. "Shall we play together? We can run down there," he added, and pointed towards a beach which lay some way from Leif's cabins. They started to run, and Magnus soon realised that he could not run as fast as the other boy.

Down on the beach they stood still for a while and Magnus looked curiously at the boy. "What's your name?" he asked. Naturally, the boy didn't understand what Magnus said and didn't reply – he just stared at him. Magnus pointed to himself and said "Magnus." Then he pointed at the boy and looked inquiringly at him. The boy's face lit up. "Maku," he said. "Maku?" repeated Magnus, and the Indian boy nodded and grinned.

From that day onwards, Magnus went into the forest each day to meet Maku, and they constantly found new and exciting things to do together. Magnus was happy. At last he had found someone to do things with. He had a friend! As the weeks wore on they became good at using their hands to explain to each other what they meant, and soon Magnus had learnt many of the words Maku used, and Maku began to understand Magnus' language.

The two boys had a great time together. They laughed about the same things and were always finding fun things to do. Both of them were inquisitive and anxious to make new discoveries, and both of them loved getting up to tricks. But they didn't dare go to Leif's cabins together, or to Maku's camp. They didn't know what the adults would do, but they were certain that they wouldn't like it.

Nevertheless, on one occasion they wandered over to the charcoal pile at Leif's cabins and hid behind some bushes, making strange noises. When the blacksmith came outside and stood listening, Maku howled like a wolf. The blacksmith was so frightened that he dropped what he was holding and rushed down towards the cabins. Magnus and Maku laughed until it hurt as they hurried back up to the forest.

One day Maku came running excitedly towards Magnus and explained in words and gestures that he had seen a wolf acting strangely. It was walking round and round as though it was looking for something. Magnus was curious, and together they ran to the place where Maku had seen the animal.

They searched high and low until they came to a small mountain ridge. Maku stopped suddenly and signalled to Magnus to stand completely still. The two boys stood glued to the spot, listening closely. As they stood there they heard a faint whimper from an injured animal. They both tiptoed forward, cautiously.

Suddenly there was fierce growl and they saw a wolf standing watching them with bared teeth and yellow, threatening eyes, ready to attack. Just in front of the wolf was a deep crevice in the rock, and from this crevice came a whimpering sound. Magnus and Maku immediately understood what must have happened – a young cub had fallen into the crevice and the mother couldn't get it out again. But they also knew that she would not allow them to come any closer!

Maku made a sign to Magnus, and slowly they drew back. Magnus' heart was in his mouth. At any moment he expected the mother to pounce on them, but she didn't move a muscle. She would not leave her cub. The boys ran back to their meeting place. Maku made a sign that they should return to help the cub when the sun had gone down below the horizon.

25

As they crept back towards the mountain ridge later that day both boys were nervous, but now there was no whimper from the crevice, and neither was the mother to be seen. Maku crept forward. He moved like an animal that had caught the scent of prey, silently and cautiously. Magnus' heart thumped in his chest. He was afraid of the furious mother wolf, but far too curious and excited to be stopped by fear. They came steadily closer while Maku kept an eye out on all sides so as not to be surprised by the mother.

Finally, they arrived at the edge of the crevice. As quick as lightning Maku jumped down into the crevice. Magnus looked anxiously about him. If the mother returned now she would attack in order to defend her cub. His hands were sweating and his mouth was dry. If only Maku would come up again soon! Magnus was so scared that he was shaking, but he never thought of running away. If Maku dared, so would he!

It seemed to take for ever, but finally the Indian boy climbed out of the crevice. In his arm he held the little wolf cub. Magnus leaned forward eagerly to take the cub. It was tiny and it whimpered pitifully, but he couldn't tell whether it was injured. Maku took the cub from him and examined it. It appeared that he was used to saving helpless animals. Then Maku smiled and signalled that everything was all right. He took the cub away from the rocks and gently placed it in the heather. He took a couple of steps backwards and made a sound like a wolf cry, and signalled to Magnus to start running.

They hid behind a large rock, and it was not long before the mother wolf returned. They were curious to see whether the mother would reject the cub since Maku had had it in his hands. But luckily, after sniffing it, she began to lick the cub. Magnus and Maku smiled at each other. They stayed behind the rock until the mother wolf and her cub had disappeared.

When Magnus was in bed later that evening, he lay there thinking about what he and Maku had done that day. He wondered whether Father and his men had ever saved a helpless wolf …

Every day that passed, Magnus learned a little more about Maku and his people. Maku told him that they did not live permanently in one place but followed the reindeer herds in summer down to the coast where they set up their tents by the river. When the reindeer returned inland during the autumn, Maku's people followed them. Maku explained that they collected eggs and caught fish, seabirds and seals, that his father hunted with a spear as well as with a bow and arrow, and that they had boats called canoes made from the bark of birch trees.

Magnus didn't think that Maku and his parents lived so very differently from his own family. The only real difference was that Maku lived in a kind of tent covered in bark, while Magnus lived in a longhouse and had cows which gave milk. Maku had never heard of this. In addition, Maku explained that his mother and the other women had to pull the sledges when they moved from one place to the next. The men only hunted. They frequently slept under their canoes. The only thing that Magnus thought was a bit strange was that Maku said that all the animals could talk and that they had an inner spirit, just like humans. It was easier to understand the things he said about good and evil spirits which existed in the trees, in the Northern Lights, in the wind, the sun and the moon. This was similar to what Olve had told him, Magnus thought.

Magnus became more and more surprised that Leif had described Maku's people as wild beings. He had also said that they were weak people, but this didn't seem right either, Magnus thought. He became increasingly impatient to tell his mother and father about Maku, but something held him back. His father and the other men often spoke about the wild people. One evening Father had found one of his men in the forest with an arrow through his heart.

One day when Magnus came home, his father told him that a horde of wild men had come charging towards Leif's cabins, but when the oxen began to bellow, they were frightened and ran away.

"What do you think they want with us?" asked Mother nervously. Father said nothing.

"They don't want us here," said one of the other men sombrely. "Last year Leif's brother and his men killed eight of these wild men who had hidden themselves under the boats." Everyone remained silent.

Mother turned towards Magnus. "You'd better stay down here near the houses, Magnus. Those wild people are dangerous."

"What a shame," she added with a deep sigh. "Everything else is so perfect here. We have plenty of food, what with the whale meat, seal meat, fish and salmon in the river. The cows can stay outside all year, and we have timber and all the berries we want. We didn't have any of those things in Greenland."

She turned to Father. "I had hoped that the children could grow up here in this land," she said, placing her hand upon her swollen tummy. How strange, thought Magnus. Inside that tummy is my little sister or brother who I will soon see for the first time. He knew that the new baby would be arriving soon.

"That they shall," said Father decisively. "We just have to find out how to keep the wild people away."

Magnus strolled over to the longhouse. Ketil Flatnose sat outside carving strange markings on a piece of wood. When Magnus asked him what it was, Ketil told him that the markings were called runes and that using these it was possible to write messages to people. Magnus wanted to know what he had written, but Ketil wouldn't tell him. "Runes are magic and secret and were created by Odin. That's why I can't tell you."

But suddenly he changed his mind and whispered in Magnus' ear. "It says 'The enemy's spear is blunted, and neither cunning nor weapons will help'."

"What does that mean?" asked Magnus.

"It means that I have the power to make the wild men's weapons powerless," replied Ketil Flatnose. Magnus thought about Maku. He felt very uncomfortable.

And then the time arrived when Magnus' little brother or sister was to come into the world, and all the women gathered at the house of Magnus' mother. Magnus was very excited throughout that long day. Late in the evening his father came to him with a broad smile on his face and told him that he now had a little brother who was to be called Snorre.

"He is the first of our people to be born in this new land in the west!" said Father proudly.

Magnus simply had to run into the forest to tell Maku about his little brother, even though Mother had told him to stay near the cabins. He would just tell him the good news and then run back home again. To his great disappointment he did not find Maku at their normal meeting place. He shouted and searched, and before he realised it, he had wandered further and further away from the cabins.

Once he thought he heard Maku's voice somewhere deep in the forest and he ran quickly towards the sound. Maku had said that his tribe had their camp down by the river bank. If he was careful and kept a keen lookout, he could follow the river downstream until he reached the camp, and then he could hide until he saw Maku. If he whistled using the secret signal they had agreed, then his friend would certainly come at once.

He simply had to find Maku, as it would soon be autumn and then the Indians would follow the wild reindeer inland and not return until the spring. Magnus felt a lump in his throat when he thought about that. Nothing would be the same without Maku!

Then he heard some strange sounds. They must be coming from Maku's camp. He ran forward eagerly. Suddenly he stopped in his tracks. Coming towards him was a group of brown men dressed in skins, with long black hair, red paint on their faces and bows and arrows in their hands. Some of them also carried long spears, and they were coming straight towards him. His heart began to pound in his chest. The men looked very angry and exceedingly dangerous. Magnus did not dare to move, his mouth was dry and his body was paralysed with fear.

Horrified, he saw the leader raise his spear, ready to cast it at him. Magnus tried to scream, but no sound came out. At that moment something happened. A scream resounded through the forest – but it did not come from Magnus. The men turned around, surprised by the sound.

Out of the bushes came Maku, running at full speed. He dashed up to the leader and called out something Magnus did not understand. The man lowered his spear, turned around and looked suspiciously at Magnus. Then he gave a sign and all the others lowered their weapons too. Maku went up to Magnus. "Go home!" he said. "Father is angry. Your men killed eight of our men last year!"

Magnus nodded sadly. "Are you leaving now?" he asked. Maku nodded. "Yes, but we will return in the spring."

Magnus hesitated a moment, but then he had to say it. "I've got a baby brother," he said quickly, and then turned and ran full speed homewards, forcing back his tears.

When he arrived back at Leif's cabins, there was an air of panic throughout the settlement. Everybody had been out searching for him.

Magnus told them everything that had happened, right from the first time that he had met Maku, how his friend had rescued the wolf cub, and how he had saved his life today. When he finished speaking there was complete silence around him. Mother lifted her hand and placed it on his head. "You are a remarkable boy, Magnus," she said quietly. "You have understood what I have been trying to learn from the White Christ." "What is that?" asked Magnus.

"That the Indians are humans just like us."

Father stood thinking for a long time, and then he said "When the Indians return in the spring, I shall find some goods and try to show them that we wish to trade with them. They do not have cows, so they could get milk from us, and clothes which we have spun and woven, and perhaps we can get some grey squirrel furs and other products from them."

Mother smiled. "Then we can be at peace with each other, and settle here in Vinland," she said with satisfaction.

"And then Maku and I can carry on being best friends," exclaimed Magnus happily.

About the Vikings

The Discovery of North America: In about AD 1000, Leif Eriksson discovered a new land in the west which we now know as North America. He called the land where he settled 'Vinland'. Later archaeological excavations showed his settlement to be at a place we now call L'Anse aux Meadows (Meadows Bay) in Newfoundland.

Leif Eriksson: Leif was the son of the powerful Norwegian Viking chief Erik the Red from south-west Norway, who established the Greenland colony. Leif grew up in Greenland. Following the discovery of Vinland, several of Leif's family travelled to the newly discovered land. Leif's brother Thorvald was the first to settle there, but he was killed by the Indians. Thorvald was followed by his wife, Gudrid, and her new husband – the Icelandic chieftain Thorfinn Karlsevne. Gudrid gave birth to a child in this new land – probably the first white child to be born on American soil.

They came from Greenland: All voyages to North America at that time started in Greenland, where people had settled from about AD 950 until AD 1400, after which the community is believed to have been destroyed by pirates. There is much to indicate that the Greenlanders continued to sail to North America throughout this period. Five hundred years after Leif Eriksson's expedition, Christopher Columbus rediscovered this new land in the west.

Vinland: The land discovered by Leif Eriksson. The name comes from the old Norse term meaning grassy area or pasture. It was a rich country. Here the settlers found forests, wild reindeer, fur-bearing animals, walruses and seals. They also found berries in large quantities which they did not have in Greenland.

The Viking era: This period lasted from approximately AD 793 until AD 1066.
Leif Eriksson discovered North America in the latter part of the Viking era. The Vikings came from Norway, Sweden and Denmark. Some were pirates, others were merchants who travelled afar in order to buy and sell products. Yet others journeyed across the seas with their families to discover new lands as there was not sufficient food at home. They travelled in large Viking ships which they sailed or rowed using many pairs of oars. At the bow of each ship was a large dragon's head to ward off evil spirits.